JUBA GOOD

JUBA
GOOD

VICKI DELANY

ORCA BOOK PUBLISHERS

Library and Archives Canada Cataloguing in Publication

Delany, Vicki, 1951–, author
Juba good / Vicki Delany.
(Rapid reads)

Issued in print and electronic formats.
ISBN 978-1-4598-0490-6 (pbk.).—ISBN 978-1-4598-0491-3 (pdf).—
ISBN 978-1-4598-0492-0 (epub)

I. Title. II. Series: Rapid reads
PS8557.E4239J82 2014   C813'.6   C2013-907626-3
C2013-907627-1

First published in the United States, 2014
Library of Congress Control Number: 2013956420

Summary: RCMP Sergeant Ray Robertson, nearing the end of his year-long UN
mission in Juba, South Sudan, struggles to find a serial killer. (RL 3.0)
A free reading guide for this title is available at rapid-reads.com.

*Orca Book Publishers is dedicated to preserving the environment and has
printed this book on Forest Stewardship Council® certified paper.*

Orca Book Publishers gratefully acknowledges the support for its publishing
programs provided by the following agencies: the Government of Canada, the
Canada Council for the Arts and the Province of British Columbia through the
BC Arts Council and the Book Publishing Tax Credit.

Design by Jenn Playford
Cover photography by plainpicture

ORCA BOOK PUBLISHERS
orcabook.com

Printed and bound in Canada.

21 20 19 18 • 5 4 3 2

For Caroline

CHAPTER ONE

I jumped out of the way of a speeding boda boda and tripped over a pregnant goat. The driver of the scooter yelled at me. I gave him a hand gesture in return. Not a good idea, in this town, at this time of night. But I'd had a rotten day and was in a matching mood.

The goat I ignored. It was not a good idea to interfere with her. She was worth money.

Juba, South Sudan. April. The dry season. The air red with dust blowing down from the desert to the north. Choking dust.

Getting into everything. Me, coughing up my lungs half the night.

At six foot three, I'm considered a big guy back home in Canada. Here, in a group of locals, I'm about average. Some of these guys—heck, some of the women—must be close to seven feet. Damn good-looking women though.

My name's Ray Robertson. In Canada, I'm an RCMP officer. In South Sudan, I'm with the UN. Our role is to be trainers, mentors and advisers. Help the new country of South Sudan build a modern police force.

Yeah, right.

I've been in the country eleven and a half months. Just over two weeks to go. First thing I'm going to do when I check into my hotel in Nairobi is have a bath. A long hot bath. Get all that red dirt out of my lily-white skin. Jenny gets in the next morning. We're going to Mombasa.

A fancy hotel. A week on the beach. Sex and warm water and clean sand. More sex. Heaven.

I climbed into the police truck. I'd recently begun working with John Deng. He was a good guy, Deng. From the Dinka tribe, so about as tall and thin as a lamp-post. He didn't say much, but what he did say was worth listening to.

His phone rang. Deng spoke into it, a couple of short words I didn't catch. He hung up and turned to me. His eyes and teeth were very white in the dark.

"Another dead woman," he said.

"Damn."

Deng put the truck into gear and we pulled into the traffic. Think you've seen traffic chaos? Come to Juba. The city's mostly dirt roads. Uncovered manholes, open drainage ditches and piles of rubble. Potholes you could lose a family in. Trucks, 4x4s, cars, boda bodas, pedestrians, goats, chickens and the occasional small child. Every one of them fighting for space, jostling to push another inch through the crowds. The roads have no street signs and few traffic signs. Which no one pays attention to anyway.

We drove toward the river. The White Nile. The goal of Burton, Speke, Baker, the great Victorian explorers. The river's wide here, moving fast. It's not white for sure. More the color of warm American beer. Full of twigs and branches and whole trees trapped in the current. Plus a lot of other things that I don't want to think much about.

The old settlement's called Juba Town. Disintegrating white buildings, cracked and broken sidewalks, mountains of rubbish. A crumbling blue mosque in a dusty square. Small shops selling anything and everything alongside outdoor markets hawking goods.

In daytime, the streets are crowded. Soldiers in green camouflage uniforms.

Police in blue camo. Adults going about their business. Bare-bottomed babies. Schoolchildren with scrubbed faces, clean uniforms and wide, friendly smiles. Honking horns, shouting men, chatting women, music and laughter.

Now, at night, all was quiet. A handful of fires burned in trash piles that had spilled into the streets. Men sat in circles drinking beer. Women watched from open doorways. Above, thick clouds blocked moon and stars.

A water station had been built close to the river. Blue water trucks lined up there during the day to get safe water. The street was a mess of deep puddles, red mud, rocks, ruts and trash. Not as good as some, better than most.

Deng stopped our truck at the bend. Where the road turned sharply to run parallel to the river. He left the vehicle lights on and we got out. I pulled my flashlight out of my belt. Flashlight and a night stick.

That's all I carried. No weapon. This was a training mission, remember. I was here to observe. To offer comments and helpful ideas when needed.

A year without the Glock, and I still felt like I had a giant hole in my side.

Deng carried an AK-47. He was former army, SPLA—Sudan People's Liberation Army. At first a band of guerillas, fighting for independence from Sudan. Now the army of South Sudan. He'd spent his time in the bush during the war, doing things I couldn't imagine. Things I didn't want to imagine. The long and brutal civil war had made these people hard. Some of them didn't handle it too well. Deng did. He had a quick smile and a hearty laugh. He wanted to be a good police officer. I'd asked him once if he had a wife and children. A mask settled over his face. He yelled at the driver of a scooter who hadn't come at all close to us. I never asked again.

The woman was lying at the side of the road, up against a concrete wall. Her skin was as black as midnight. Blacker. An earring made of red glass hung from her right ear. A short tight black dress and red stilettos were clues to her occupation. Another dead hooker in the dusty red streets of Juba.

This was the fourth. If she was a hooker. If the same person had been responsible. The fourth in three weeks.

Deng snarled at the security guard who'd found her. The man quickly stepped back. He knew his place.

I used my Maglite to illuminate the scene. A white ribbon was wrapped around her neck. Wrapped very tightly around her neck. As white and pure as the snow on Kokanee Glacier in midwinter. Same as the others.

"What do you see?" I asked Deng. That's the training part of my job.

"A white ribbon."

"Yup."

"Do we have a serial killer here, Ray?"

"I'm beginning to think we do."

CHAPTER TWO

Forensic rules of evidence tend to be a bit wobbly in South Sudan. We wouldn't be joined by a crew of techs in hairnets and white booties. No police tape. No fingertip search of the vicinity. No lab analysis. No DNA samples taken. No databases checked for similar cases. The body would be carted away and that would be the end of that.

Deng and I did what we could to examine the scene.

It looked as if she'd been taken by surprise. Strangled with the white ribbon.

Left where she fell. No defensive wounds
on her hands or arms. No signs of sexual
activity.

Deng crouched down. "What does the
ribbon mean?" He reached out one hand
and ran his fingers over it very lightly.

"I don't know. It means something
to him. He might not even know what.
Sometimes they leave a sign. Sometimes
they take trophies."

"Trophies?"

"Yeah. I don't see anything missing
here. Serial killers usually have a signature.
His is the white ribbon."

Deng shook his head. When you've
seen so much death and dying, it's hard to
believe someone would do it for...fun?

At a guess—and it would never be more
than a guess—she'd been dead about two
hours. Not many bugs yet. No rigor mortis.

I'd once tried to explain rigor mortis to
Deng and his colleagues. They'd nodded

very politely. I'd felt like a total fool. These guys had seen more dead bodies than any undertaker in Vancouver. They knew the process of decay, thank you very much.

Sometimes they could be so goddamned polite. Why didn't they just tell me to shut the hell up? Suggest we take the time allocated for the lecture to go for a beer?

Deng and I shone our flashlights around the area. I made notes in my notebook. And then we left. What else could we do? The carcass would be loaded into the back of a van and that would be the end of her.

The bend in the road was close to Notos. A good bar with a great Indian kitchen. I suggested we stop in for a drink. Deng looked surprised. We UN advisors told them drinking on the job was a bad thing. I winked and said it was all part of the job.

Which wasn't a lie.

Notos was a popular spot. Aid workers and foreign government staffers hung out there.

They might have seen something. The rest of the road was made up of tin shacks and cardboard houses. Plus a few of the traditional mud and grass huts called tukuls. No one there would help the police.

The fire in the pizza oven blazed. Spices filled the air. The bar hopped with good jazz.

The restaurant was full. I nodded to a couple of Canadian embassy staff. We went to the bar. I ordered two orange Fantas. Deng tried not to look too terribly disappointed.

The bartender was named Shirley. A knockout in a neat white shirt and black pants, with short-cropped black hair. She passed the bottles over with a soft smile. The smile was directed not at me but at Deng. He didn't seem to notice.

"Busy tonight," I said.

"Usual."

"Some trouble out on the street earlier. A couple of hours ago. Maybe around nine. Did you hear anything, Shirley?"

She glanced at Deng from under her eyelashes.

He said, "Did you?"

"Can't hear anything over the noise in here."

"Did anyone go out for a break, maybe? Smoke. Get some air?"

A silent shake of her head. She slid down to the end of the bar to take an order.

That's the problem with policing here. You don't know what experiences people have had. In Canada, we get suspicious if someone avoids police questions. Most people want to be helpful. Whether they have anything to be helpful about or not. But here, with the trauma some of these people have experienced?

Maybe they're as guilty as sin.

Maybe they don't much care.

Maybe they've seen men in uniform slaughter whole families.

You just don't know.

I visited the tables. I asked the same questions I'd asked Shirley. Got nothing but shakes of the head and questions back.

Only a shy young waitress named Marlene thought hard. I suspected Marlene liked me. I didn't know if she really liked me or was just hoping for a visa to Canada. I made sure to always keep things light and no more than friendly. Tonight, she had nothing to say that would help us.

Back to the bar. I leaned against the counter and sucked on my Fanta. The restaurant was emptying out. People called good night to their friends in the warm night air.

A tall white woman, blond, pretty, came up to the bar. She dug in her purse. "I need more Internet time," she said. "Can I buy three hours?" Her English was perfect, the Dutch accent strong. She gave me a smile as Shirley searched for the Internet vouchers. I hadn't seen the Dutch woman when we came through the restaurant.

"Do you live nearby?" I asked.

"In the townhouses, yes." Four modern townhouses were next to the restaurant. They were surrounded by a concrete wall. They boasted a rare patch of scrappy lawn and trimmed bushes.

"Were you outside earlier? Say around nine, ten?"

"Why do you ask?"

"Police business."

Deng refrained from rolling his eyes. He thought I was trying to pick her up.

She laughed through a mouthful of perfect white teeth. "I had dinner with friends. Came home by taxi. Around nine, I think. What happened?"

"There was a killing. On the corner. Where the road bends."

She lifted her hand to her mouth. "A killing? Who? Someone I know?"

"A local, probably."

The concern faded from her face. "That's very sad."

"It might have been around that time. Did you see anything unusual?"

She hesitated.

"What?" I asked, my tone sharper than I'd intended.

Shirley passed her a slip of paper. "Twenty-five pounds."

The Dutch woman handed over an orange bill. She chewed her lip. "I heard something."

"Yes?"

"The air-conditioning wasn't working in the taxi. The windows were down. I heard someone—a woman—scream."

"And?"

"And nothing. Just a scream. Once only." She looked away, embarrassed.

"We drove on, and I heard no more. I'm sorry." She scurried off.

I let out a long sigh.

"What did you expect, Ray?" Deng asked.

A good question. I expected nothing else, really. No one would want to get involved. Not many people would much care. What was the scream of a woman in the hot African night?

In Canada, plenty of people would have rolled up their windows too.

"Helps narrow the time," I said, not very helpfully. "The state of the body indicated a time of death around nine. The scream was heard at that time."

"Very helpful," Deng said. I suspected he was being sarcastic.

I put the remains of my sickly sweet orange drink on the bar and stalked out. Deng followed, chuckling.

CHAPTER THREE

Home sweet container.

I live in a shipping container in the UN compound. The walls are painted a practical beige. It has no art, no decorations, no rugs. In my good moods, I think of it as my man cave. The single bed's moderately comfortable. The small desk has a flimsy office chair and a laptop.

It has plumbing and electricity. But it's still a box.

Three pictures sit on the night table. Our eldest daughter at her wedding.

Our second daughter at her university graduation. Jenny and me at our wedding. Looking so young, so happy. I had long curly hair back then. Not much of it's left these days.

I didn't sleep well that night. Not that it was night when I crawled into bed. The hot sun was rising in the eastern sky.

I've seen a lot in my time as a cop. More than I like to think about sometimes. Not much bothers me anymore, unless it's kids. I hate it when violence is done to kids.

But I couldn't get the dead hooker out of my mind. She might not have even been a hooker. These days it's hard to tell the hookers from the office workers out for a night on the town with their girlfriends.

The woman looked to be South Sudanese. These people had been through so much hardship. If the woman was in her twenties, chances were she'd never known anything but civil war.

Then to be killed, murdered, in a time of peace.

Life could be so damn unfair.

* * *

I rolled out of bed not long after noon. I pulled on white shorts and a Vancouver Canucks T-shirt and went in search of breakfast.

The UN compound is close to the center of Juba. It's clean and tidy, with a bit of grass and some flowering bushes. Neatly swept footpaths and small houses with curtains in the windows.

Surrounded by concrete walls topped with razor wire.

Step out the gate and you're in Africa.

I crossed the yard. The air was an orange haze. Everything was covered with dust. It hadn't rained since October. Everyone was waiting, waiting, for the first rains of the season to fall and the heat to break.

The sun wasn't visible through the murk. But I always wore a broad-brimmed beige hat to protect my balding head.

Two people were in the common room when I entered. Joyce, a tall lean Australian with a shock of wild red hair, was in uniform. She was eating eggs and reading. She lifted her head, said hi and returned to her food and book. Peter, a cop from Namibia, was sprawled across the badly sprung couch, watching TV. As always, a soccer game was on. I hate soccer. Give me a good hockey game any day. Even baseball's better than soccer. But they sure love soccer in Africa.

I popped two slices of bread into the toaster. I twisted open the top of a jar of peanut butter. On the TV, the crowd roared. I didn't bother to look up. No one would have scored. No one ever scores in soccer. They run around the field for two hours and then have a shoot-out to decide the winner.

Might as well just have the shoot-out and everyone go home early. I grunted in disapproval.

"Something bothering you, man?" Peter asked.

My toast popped up. I began spreading a thick layer of peanut butter. Love peanut butter.

The door opened. Orange dust blew in along with Nigel, a Brit. A short, bald, pasty-faced guy, arms and chest thick with muscle.

Nigel grunted greetings and headed straight for the fridge. He pulled out a can of Coke. "A killing last night," I said, answering Peter's question. "A woman. Down by the river."

Joyce looked up. "Raped?"

"No sign of it. It's the fourth one like it this month."

Her mouth twisted and she shook her head. She glanced at her watch.

"I gotta go. Fill me in later." She folded down the corner of a page and got to her feet. She stuffed the book into her pocket.

"Hooker?" Peter asked as the door slammed shut after Joyce. His eyes remained fixed on the TV.

"Probably."

"Occupational hazard."

I felt a tightening in my gut. "Even a cheap hooker doesn't deserve to be slaughtered like a pig."

"Then she shouldn't be hooking."

"They don't always have a choice, you know." Nigel took out a second can. "Husband dead, family to support."

"Save it, mate," Peter said. "I've heard it all before. Hooking's easier than working in a shop or washing dishes. Pay's better too. I've got no tears for them."

I'd heard it all before too. The threat of rape or murder shouldn't be part of the job. No matter what type of job it is.

But I didn't feel like arguing. I ate my toast.

I went back to my container. I had a long-standing tennis date with a Dutch diplomat named Donald.

I grabbed my racket and headed out.

My room was next to Sven's, a cop from Sweden. Sven was sitting on a plastic chair in the shade of a mango tree. Barely past noon and he was already sucking on a brown bottle.

But he wasn't working, so not my concern.

"Morning," I said. Just to be friendly.

He grunted. Typical.

I stopped in front of him. I told him about the killing the night before. Asked him to keep an eye out when he was next on patrol.

"Never would have thought of that," he said. "Is that what they consider in Canada to be an original idea?"

I didn't rise to the bait. "Just mentioning it. Ask your partner to be on the lookout too."

"Yeah, we'll look out for hookers. Keep them all nice and safe." He took another slug of his beer.

I walked away. I sometimes wondered why Sven had taken this post. He hid it well, but he didn't seem overly fond of Africans. Nor of women, come to think of it.

Most of the guys and the few women posted here get on fine. They're a good bunch of people. Gave up career and family for a year to try to help a struggling country. We're all far from home, living in rough conditions. We try hard to make it work. But there's one in every bunch. Sven was ours.

As usual, Donald whipped my ass at tennis. Instead of our usual beer after the game, Donald had to leave for a meeting. I planned to head back to the UN compound.

I'd grab an early supper and read for a while. Then it would be time to meet Deng for another night on the streets.

Instead, I found myself driving to the police station near the water tanks.

The place was barely controlled chaos. I'd found in my time here that things might look out of control, but somehow they made it work. Juba good, we call it.

I knew the clerk at the front desk. He sat at a large black ledger, making note of anyone who came in with a complaint or an inquiry. Not many did.

"Hi, Edward," I said. "Busy?"

"Yes," he replied. There wasn't a civilian in sight. Most of the police here knew me, and they paid me no attention.

"A woman was killed last night," I said. "Has anyone come in asking about her?"

Edward shrugged. I glanced at his book. The surface was unmarked. He didn't bother to flip back through the pages to check.

His cell phone rang, and he pulled it out of his shirt pocket. He began to talk.

I leaned across him and turned the book around. I flipped the page. The latest entry had been at noon yesterday.

I should have known I was wasting my time. I left the building. I sat in the UN SUV, air-conditioning running hard, and thought. I could try the hospital. If anyone was looking for the dead woman, they'd be more likely to go there than to the cops.

I decided I couldn't face it. Let her be. If no one else cared, why should I?

CHAPTER FOUR

But I've never been good at letting things go. Instead of heading home, I drove to the bend in the road. Blue water trucks were lined up around the corner, waiting their turn. The drivers squatted by the side of the road or stood in groups, gossiping. I left my vehicle at Notos and walked over. The workers and drivers paid no attention to me.

Garbage collection is an unknown concept in much of Africa. Scraps of paper blew in the dusty wind. Cardboard floated in the red puddles. Water bottles were stacked against walls where the wind had left them. I reached the spot where we'd found the woman. I squatted and pulled on a pair of latex gloves—to protect me, not the evidence. I poked through trash, leaves and twigs. I found a handle broken off a cooking pot and the leavings of stray dogs.

Then a flash of color caught my eye. I pulled a glittering red earring out of the rubbish. Glass. I thought back. Yes, the dead woman had been wearing one, and only one, red earring. I slipped it into my pocket. I started to push myself back up. A white square caught my eye. A business card, the sort you'd find anywhere in the world. Reasonably clean with a smudge of red dust in one corner. It hadn't been there for long.

The card was for Blue Nile Restaurant. A place on the river, with tent fabric for roof and walls. It serves Middle Eastern food, mostly. I've been there once. I didn't care for the cooking and never went back.

I tucked the card into my pocket beside the red earring. Then I went home to get ready for work.

CHAPTER FIVE

The main road through Juba features a row of streetlights. Good solid streetlights of the sort you'd see in any western city. Tonight, some drunk had found out just how solid they were.

By the time we got to the scene, the crowd of onlookers was growing. The car, a battered old Toyota Corolla, was buried headfirst in the base of a lamppost. The driver was buried headfirst in the dashboard. He had not bothered to put on his seat belt. Nor had his female companion. She was now little more than a bloody lump thirty yards farther up the road. The car was about twenty years old and did not come equipped with air bags. It might well have been stolen off a lot in Vancouver.

I told Deng we were here to do crowd control until the bodies were carted away. We would try to keep the curious from going through the wreck and the pockets of the deceased.

Shame about that streetlight. It would have cost a lot, in a country that didn't have much to spend on luxuries.

A van arrived and the bodies were loaded up. Then everyone drifted away, and Deng and I got back into our truck. An old woman came out of nowhere and began sweeping the road with a homemade broom.

The rest of the night was quiet.

The next day, I decided to treat myself to lunch out. Back home, I have a reputation for being quite the good cook. When the kids were growing up and my shifts permitted,

I did most of the cooking. Jenny's a practical cook. Meat and potatoes, lots of pasta and hearty stews. I like to try new and different things. I love nothing more than to have dinner parties. To dress up, put out the good china and make my favorite recipes.

Here, I soon learned that fresh meat is something you don't want to buy. It hangs in the market in the sun for hours, pecked by birds and covered in flies. Edible fresh greens are nonexistent. Every once in a while the grocers run right out of something. Last month, there wasn't a pat of butter to be found for love nor money anywhere in Juba.

The avocados here are great though, huge and as soft as butter. I eat a lot of avocados. Also a lot of peanut butter on white bread. I might even start to like white bread someday.

Today, I figured I deserved a treat. A late lunch at a nice place down by the river.

I signed out a car and drove to the Blue Nile.

The parking lot was mostly empty. The guard glanced at me as I drove in but otherwise didn't bother to stir himself from his hut.

The wind was high, and tent fabric rustled in the breeze. I took a table by the water, taking care to stay away from a grove of mango trees. Flying mangos can do real damage. Young boys, all skin and bones and gigantic eyes, snatched the fruit. A guard shouted at them to get away. Two women from the kitchen moved through the trees, picking mangos off the ground.

My waitress was a short woman with dark brown, not black, skin. A foreign worker, likely Ugandan. She gave me a smile that didn't touch her eyes. I ordered a beer and Nile perch with rice. It was nice in the shade, so I took off my hat.

When she brought the drink, I said, "I'm looking for a woman."

A touch of disdain filled her eyes. I added quickly, "A particular woman, I mean. She might work here." I described the dead woman. I pulled the red earring out of my pocket.

Something flashed across her face. She lowered her eyes. She shook her head and scurried away.

Past lunchtime, the restaurant was empty. A group of men, a mix of white and brown, sat at the bar. Judging by the noise, they'd been here for quite a while.

A different waitress brought my food. I described the dead woman. I got the same shake of the head and quick departure.

The beer was cold and the fish perfectly cooked. I watched the traffic on the river. Rickety rowboats, homemade canoes, a raft with a sail that might once have been a bedsheet, a rusty barge. A kayak rounded the corner. I recognized the two people paddling. Canadians who worked at the embassy. I grinned. Canadians and their canoes.

They were moving fast with the current, paddling more to steer than to provide speed. The kayak rounded the bend and disappeared.

"Can I get you anything more?" the waitress asked.

"No, thanks. Just the bill."

We looked up at a burst of laughter from the bar. The female bartender had turned away from the men, her pretty face set in angry lines. My waitress threw the men a scowl that would curdle milk.

I put my money on the table, pinning it down with a salt shaker. I put my hat on my head and walked over to the bar. I stood at the far end from the group of drinkers. The bartender asked me what I wanted.

"Just to ask a question," I said. I tried to sound friendly and not at all threatening. Again I described the dead woman and showed the earring. Again I got a negative reply. She hurried back to her customers.

I wandered around to the back of the building, following signs to the washrooms. I found them, and the kitchen, at the end of a dirt path.

Not being at all shy, I stuck my head in the kitchen door. Two men were resting on plastic stools, chatting. Their eyes widened at the sight of me.

"Hi," I said. "I'm looking for someone who works here. Maybe you know her." Again I described the dead woman. I showed the earring.

"What are you doing in here?" an angry voice said behind me. I turned to see a man with short brown hair and a brown goatee. His cheeks were round and his chin wobbled. His skin was tanned the color of old leather. The permanent tan that meant a life spent in hot places.

"Ray Robertson. I'm with the UN, assigned to assist the local police."

"I don't care who you are, mate. Get the hell out of my kitchen."

"I'm..."

"You're bothering my staff, is what you're doing. The girls complained about you. Get lost, and don't come back."

That took me aback. The staff had nothing to complain about. Maybe they didn't like my question. Maybe their boss didn't like my question.

"This is a police investigation." I tried to sound as if I had some authority here.

"Rubbish. You're just interfering. Get out."

"She's South Sudanese. Very pretty. I think this belongs to her." I pulled the earring out of my pocket.

"I've never seen that piece of junk before. You'd better not be implying I run a whorehouse here."

"I'm not implying anything. I'm asking a simple question."

"I'm answering it. Get the hell out of my place."

"Maybe you've seen her," I said. Sometimes I don't know when to quit.

With a roar, he came at me. I'd seen his intention in his eyes the moment before he moved. I ducked. I heard the air move as his fist flew past my face.

The cooks leapt to their feet and scattered. My waitress stood in the doorway. Her eyes were round and white in her dark face. She screamed.

I came back swinging. The man squealed. He tried to get out of the way, but he was too slow. Not used to hitting someone who would fight back, I thought.

I landed a solid punch in the middle of his flabby belly. He gasped, let out a puff of air and bent over. I stepped back, startled at what I'd done.

Then strong arms were on mine. I was marched out of the kitchen. Two security guards. Tall and lean. The sort of leanness that means hard and fast. They didn't try to beat me up or sneak in a punch or two. Just frog-marched me down the path to the parking lot. They shoved me against my vehicle and then stood back, watching me. They hadn't said a word.

"I get the point," I said. A gust of wind ruffled my hair. Of which I don't have much. I'd lost my hat in the scuffle. I liked that hat. The guards turned and walked away.

The little waitress came running down the path. She waved my hat toward the guards. They nodded and she approached me. Keeping her eyes down, she held the hat out.

"Thank you," I said.

"I know her," she said, her voice very low. "Judy. She works here, in the kitchen, washing dishes. At night, sometimes she comes back. With men. Men like"—she tossed her head toward the bar—"those ones."

She slipped away. I got into my car and drove home.

CHAPTER SIX

I had that night off. I'd arranged to meet some visiting Canadian army guys at Notos for dinner.

The place was packed when I arrived. Shirley was behind the bar. Jazz was playing. Cooks tended fires. Waitresses carried trays of food. Spices filled the warm night air. Jake and Ron waved when they saw me come in. They already had bottles of local beer open in front of them. Marlene greeted me with a wide smile and took my order. I thought how different this place was from the Blue Nile.

Two men sat at the table next to ours, devouring pizza. One man was as white as a piece of paper. He had pale blond hair and eyes the color of Arctic ice. The other was jet black. The black man said something and the white one laughed.

Maybe this country had promise after all.

We ordered our food and were catching up on the news when a group of six men arrived. They swaggered in, puffed up with their own self-importance. Government officials. I recognized two senior police officers.

Marlene rushed to serve them. Her real smile was gone, replaced with a tight one. A flash of fear filled her warm brown eyes.

The men made a big show of laughing too loud, shouting for drinks. One of them put his hand on Marlene's ample butt. She flinched but did not pull away.

"Little Hitlers," Jake muttered into his beer. "The curse of Africa."

We went back to our food and conversation.

"Morning comes early," Ron said at last. He waved for the bill.

The restaurant had largely emptied out. After making sure we all knew how important they were, the hotshots had quieted down. They kept Marlene on the go. I hoped they'd leave her a big tip. But I doubted it. Not unless they wanted something in return. Something more than good food and friendly service.

Jake and Ron started counting out their money. I saw the guy who'd been free with his hands push himself away from the table. He'd been watching Marlene most of the night. Now she was disappearing into the back, loaded down with dirty dishes.

The big man stood up and followed. The kitchen, I knew, was not in the same direction as the washrooms.

"Be right back," I said.

The kitchen was accessed by an outside path. This is common in places where you don't often worry about rain. And never about sleet or snow. The building was on one side of the path. A high concrete wall topped with razor wire was on the other.

I stood in the dark, listening.

A squeal of surprise. A soft grunt. Then a low cry, cut off.

"We're leaving now," I said loudly. I rounded the corner. "I wanted to say 'bye."

The big man had tiny Marlene pressed up against the wall. His knee was between her legs and his right hand over her mouth.

"Gee, sorry," I said, "Did I interrupt something?"

He stepped back. Marlene ducked out from under his arm. She adjusted her shirt, which had become untucked. "Ray!" she said brightly. "I'll be right with you."

She fled back to the lights of the bar.

The man looked at me. He said nothing.

"Have a nice evening," I said.

I went back to our table. I suggested Jake and Ron have another beer.

After a couple of minutes, the big man returned. He was strutting and laughing too loudly. He did not sit down, and he and his friends soon left.

CHAPTER SEVEN

The encounter between Marlene and the government official played on my mind for a night. Sure, attempted rape happens anywhere. Far too often. But it bothered me that he'd try it in a public place. With a table of his pals a few feet away. Little Hitlers, indeed. It didn't look good for democracy if the people were afraid of the officials.

Over the next few days, I pretty much forgot about it, as well as the murdered women. My departure and holiday with Jenny were fast approaching.

But I couldn't forget for long. A few nights after the incident at Notos, I was again on patrol with Deng. We got a call. Another one.

A woman. Body dumped in the same place. A white ribbon around her neck.

In Canada, we'd stake out the site. Maybe we'd dangle a couple of police-women as bait. But here, they just didn't have the manpower. Or, probably, much interest in a bunch of dead hookers.

Then again, I couldn't be too quick to judge. Police in Vancouver had ignored reports of missing Native women for a long time.

A security guard stood by the side of the road, waiting for us. Deng and I climbed out of the truck, and we all shook hands. Then the guard gestured to the body. It lay face down in the dust, against the wall. She was South Sudanese, six feet or more tall and very slim. She was dressed for a night out, in a flowered yellow blouse and flowing blue skirt. I thought the outfit was quite pretty.

Deng grunted.

She wore one high-heeled shoe.

Deng pointed to the other a few feet away.

The white ribbon around her neck fluttered in the breeze.

This time something was different. The ribbon wasn't tied killing-tight. And a knife was stuck into her back.

Deng and I crouched on either side of the body. Blood soaked the beautiful yellow blouse and the ground around her. Dogs and bugs would have a feast tonight.

"Tell me what this means, Ray," Deng said.

"At a guess, she saw what was coming and tried to get away. He panicked and lashed out. Or maybe he's not having enough fun strangling them anymore. I don't know."

"Bad business," the security guard said.

I looked up at him. "Did you hear anything? See anything?"

"No."

"Are you sure? It happened not long ago." At a guess, she hadn't been dead for more than an hour.

"I was at my post." He managed to sound insulted. "I saw nothing. I heard nothing. It is not my job to watch the street."

My knee protested as I pushed myself back up. I went to the truck and found a plastic shopping bag. It wasn't a proper evidence bag, but it would do.

I leaned over the woman. I pulled the knife out. It came away easily. Not much blood flowed with it. I held the knife up for Deng to see. It was long and not particularly sharp. But sharp enough. A kitchen knife. The sort you'd use to cut up a piece of tough meat before tossing it into the pot.

I signaled to Deng to flip her over. Sightless eyes stared up at us. "Have you seen this woman before?" I asked the guard.

"No."

I thanked him for calling us. He ambled away, back to his post.

I briefly wondered if the guard had killed the woman. To give him something to do on a long, boring night.

I didn't feel like stuffing the body into the truck to take it away. Instead, I told Deng to phone one of his colleagues to come and do it. Trainer's privilege, I call it.

Deng made the call. Then he said, "Always this place. Why, Ray?"

"Like the meaning of the ribbon, I don't know. Something to do with water, maybe."

Deng looked around. This was, after all, a residential street. Most of the houses might be made of tin and cardboard, but people lived in them.

He didn't have to ask why the killer didn't take the women, or their bodies, out of town. South Sudan is a post-conflict society. Still heavily militarized. Still at war with its former masters to the north.

Anyone driving out of the city at night had a good chance of being stopped. Probably detained.

I pushed myself to my feet. My knees creaked. "Let's see what we can find out."

Deng's eyebrows rose.

"Maybe someone saw something this time." I doubted we'd learn anything, but Deng needed to learn some interview skills.

We worked our way up the street. A guard was posted at the offices of a Japanese business on the corner. Also at Notos and the townhouse complex. People were still awake. Squatting in the dust or resting in plastic chairs by their cooking fires. Dirty-faced children pointed at me, laughed and called, "Khawaja." White person.

I smiled back. I asked their parents questions.

No one had seen anything. I suspected a couple of the guards had been asleep at the time.

Finally, I knocked on the door of one of the townhouses. We could hear music playing and people laughing inside. Deng muttered something about wasting time. A man opened the door a crack. When he saw me, he relaxed slightly. I wear my RCMP uniform shirt to work. A UN patch is sewn on the sleeve.

The man greeted us in a plummy British accent. "Help you?" The door opened a bit farther.

"I hope so." I asked if he'd seen any sort of trouble outside an hour or two earlier.

"No. I've guests, so I've been at home fixing dinner."

"Could I speak to your guests?"

"Sure." He stepped back and invited us in.

It was a mixed-race group of six people, men and women. They held crystal wine-glasses and sat around a large table. Candles and white linen napkins and china. A tray of soft cheeses, crackers and chutney was in the center of the table. Plus a bowl of mixed nuts. I almost drooled.

Instead, I asked my question.

One woman nodded. "I might have." She was the color of milky coffee and had an American accent. She held a wine glass in long thin fingers. "It was around nine. I'd been held up at work and was late getting here. I saw a car pulled over. Against the wall, at the bend in the road."

"Can you describe it?"

"A Land Cruiser. White. I remember thinking that was odd. There's nothing there. Not in the nighttime, when the water trucks aren't lining up. No one would park there."

My heart sped up. That familiar feeling I never get tired of. "Notice anything about it? A name, maybe? License plate prefix?" Most of the NGO vehicles have the name of the group printed on the side. Many have a symbol of a gun with a red line through it—no weapons on board. Some NGOs have special plates. Government vehicle plates begin with *GOSS*. The army's say *SPLA*.

She thought some more. She shook her head. "Sorry. No. Nothing."

"Did you see anyone inside the car? Or around it?"

"No. I'm sorry. It was dark. I wouldn't have noticed except for the damage to the back."

North America or Africa. Sometimes it could be like pulling teeth.

"What sort of damage?"

"To the rear bumper. On the left side. It was twisted. Some of it bent in and some sticking out. Like it had been rear-ended. I remember because that's what my car looked like after someone ran into me in LA."

"Thanks." I scribbled my cell number on the back of my card. My RCMP one with a phone number in BC. I handed it to her. "Call me, please, if you remember anything more."

"Sure."

"What happened, Sergeant?" the Brit asked.

I didn't bother to answer as Deng and I showed ourselves out.

"That was good policing, Ray," Deng said. "Let us go out and find a white Land Cruiser with a damaged bumper." He laughed heartily, teeth white in his black face in the black night.

"Shut up," I said.

There are hundreds—thousands—of white Land Cruisers in Juba. I'd be surprised if any of them *didn't* have damage.

"It's all part of building a case," I said. "You never know what's going to be impor-tant until it is important."

I wasn't fooling even myself.

CHAPTER EIGHT

Coincidences do happen. But they're rare.

I was making breakfast the next morning. Nigel came into the common room.

"Hear about Sven's car?" he asked, chuckling.

"No. What happened?"

"Stolen."

"When?"

"Last night. Fool couldn't get parking in front of a restaurant. He left the car around the corner." Meaning out of sight of the restaurant guards. "Gone when he got back."

"He musta been pissed."

"Oh, yeah. In more ways than one." Nigel chuckled. "It was his own vehicle."

My toast popped up. I ignored it. Sven had bought a used car. Fixing up old cars was his hobby, he'd said. "Remind me again what it looked like."

Nigel laughed. "What, you're going to put out an APB? Get real, Robertson. You're too keen for your own good. You're not getting any brownie points for being a good copper here, you know."

"You've got nothing to do today?" I said.

"As little as I can get away with." He took a Coke out of the fridge and left.

Peter was in his usual place. In front of the TV, watching soccer.

"It was a white Land Cruiser," he said. "Sven bought it from an NGO, painted over the logo."

"What sort of condition was it in?"

He shrugged. "Not bad. Had been in an accident. Rear-ended, I think. But the engine was good."

"Is Sven around?"

Peter laughed. "He's got no place to go, does he? And no way to get there."

Sven was sitting in his plastic garden chair when I walked up to his container. He glowered at me. He didn't lower his sunglasses. His pale blue eyes hurt in the glare of the African sun.

"What do you want, Robertson?"

"Heard about your vehicle. Stolen, eh?"

"You find it?"

"No."

"What business is it of yours then?"

It was no secret that he and I didn't get along. Didn't bother me. Sven didn't get on with many people. Not even his fellow Swedes.

"I had an incident last night. An unmarked white Land Cruiser might have been involved. What time was yours taken?"

"Early. Around seven. Barely dark. I was going to meet some friends at the rugby game later. Had dinner, came out, my car was gone." I don't speak Swedish, but I know a string of curses when I hear one.

"Who'd you have dinner with?"

Sven lowered his sunglasses. Piercing blue eyes trimmed with pale lashes studied me. He searched for a reason to tell me to get lost. Not finding one, he said, "My date canceled. I ate alone. I like to be alone. Get it?"

I got it. I left him stewing. angry

I went back to my room to check my email, hoping for something from my daughters. It was entirely possible Sven's vehicle had been stolen. Leaving it out of sight of the restaurant guards had been a dumb move.

If that's what had happened.

But what if it hadn't been stolen? What if Sven had to ditch it for some reason?

Like the passenger seat was full of blood.

CHAPTER NINE

The sixth killing came two days later. The same as the others. No sign of sexual interference. A white ribbon around the neck. But this time, there was something very different. The tips of two of the fingers on her right hand had been chopped off.

By now, even the brass couldn't ignore the fact that we had a serial killer on our hands. I told them we needed men on this. They gave me three. Ex-SPLA. Young guys with old eyes. They smiled at me and saluted smartly.

I had them do a search near where the body had been found. It was farther down the road this time, close to where a path leads through the bush to the banks of the Nile. I strung some rope between bushes and fenceposts to secure the area.

An excited crowd gathered to watch. The adults were good to stay out of the search zone. I couldn't do much about the dogs and goats and chickens though. And I had to allow parents through to chase after laughing toddlers.

We call a detailed sweep of a specific area a fingertip search. This time, the term was meant literally.

I wanted her body parts. If the killer had a fetish, he would have been taking trophies before this. There had to be a reason he'd taken the fingers. I was guessing it was because his blood was on them.

At home, I'd assume the killer knew we could get DNA evidence from blood traces.

We'd run a computer search for matching DNA. He'd know he had to get rid of the evidence.

But here? Would a local know that?

He would if he watched TV or movies. Or read a modern detective novel. People who live in the countryside, and many in town, don't have electricity. But they still have access to TV and DVDs. Many South Sudanese and other Africans can read English as well as I can. Plenty of government and army high-ups have been educated in Cuba or the west.

Shows on TV give the impression that getting DNA evidence is fast and easy. It's not. You need a fully equipped lab, trained staff and a connected computer network. Otherwise, all you have is a drop of blood. Not usable information.

I looked around. The police officers were sifting through garbage. They were being trained by the UN. They'd know something about DNA. But probably not much.

My men found a lot of plastic water bottles, scraps of cloth, discarded packaging and rotting vegetable peels. They did not find the tips of any fingers.

I had one week until I was done here. On my way home. I wanted this guy. I wanted him dead or in jail before I left.

I was afraid I'd never find out what happened.

I instructed my men to ask questions. I didn't expect much. Deng and I went back to the main police station. I intended to make more noise. → complain

We drove by the prison. It is a truly hellish place. A landscape of concrete walls, plastic bags caught in razor wire, weeds and scrub brush. Wary-eyed guards toting AK-47s.

A skinny white guy was standing on the cracked sidewalk outside the prison. I glanced at him as we drove by. I shouted at Deng to stop the car. The damn fool was taking a camera out of his backpack.

I leapt out of the truck, yelling, "Put that away."

He blinked at me. His glasses were thick and streaked with dust. "What?"

"Put that camera away. Unless you want to see what's inside that building."

Guards began to pay attention. One of them swung his rifle off his shoulder. He walked toward us. Deng called to him in a language I didn't understand.

"Now!" I yelled.

The man stuffed the camera away. "I just wanted a picture," he whined.

"Why are you here?"

"I'm out for a walk."

"I mean here. In Juba."

"I'm visiting a friend."

"Didn't your friend tell you not to take pictures? Not when there are soldiers or police around."

"He said no pictures of the military. I thought that meant like tanks and bases and stuff. What is that building anyway?"

"Hope you never find out. Get going. I'll tell that guy I know you."

He seemed to finally understand that I wasn't kidding. He hurried away. He glanced over his shoulder every few yards. He couldn't have looked more guilty.

Deng said something and the prison guard looked at me. He laughed heartily.

Then he and Deng shook hands and he went back to his post.

Most of the police and security guards here are ex-army. Many suffer from untreated PTSD. One of the symptoms of PTSD is paranoia. Distrust of anyone and everyone. It is forbidden to take pictures of anything official. They decide what is official.

I know of a woman who got in trouble for taking photos of the big-horned cows in the cattle pens. If that guy had been caught photographing the prison, of all things, I wouldn't want to be in his shoes.

I climbed back into the truck. Deng said nothing. I'm sure he thinks we white people are all crazy.

We took seats in the police station. We waited for someone to agree to see us. A man came storming through the doors. He was Indian, short and thin. He had thick black hair and blazing black eyes.

He began yelling about a stolen car. My ears pricked up.

I went over and introduced myself. It wasn't easy, but I got him calmed down enough to tell me his story.

He'd been visiting a friend. His eyes shifted, and I could guess at the nature of this friendship. Not my business. When he'd come out of his friend's apartment this morning, his car was gone.

Stolen. Right from under the noses of the building's guards. I took the description of the vehicle. He ranted and raved for a few minutes. I told him someone would be with him shortly. Then I signaled to Deng and we left.

"What?" Deng said once we were outside. He was getting good at reading me.

"Stolen cars. There's a connection, I'm sure of it. He's stealing a car and using it to transport the women."

"One stolen car doesn't make a pattern, Ray."

I hadn't told him about Sven. I decided to keep that under my hat for a while.

The question was, had the thefts been followed by the murders all along? Or did that start when the killer had to ditch his own vehicle?

CHAPTER TEN

I decided I didn't much care that the boss was too busy to see us. Our shift was over and I wanted to head home. On the way, we spotted a crowd forming at the side of the road. Deng pulled over.

A small black man was standing beside a new SUV. His back was pressed up against the car door. Two light-skinned brown women peered out the windows. The man must be their driver. A police officer was yelling at the small man. The officer waved his finger in the air. He was about a foot taller and a hundred pounds heavier than the driver.

I was out of the truck before Deng had fully stopped. I pushed my way through the chattering crowd. People called to me. They said there'd been an accident. I didn't see another car or anyone hurt.

It was a shakedown, probably. The women looked like NGO or embassy employees. The driver was Kenyan or Ugandan.

"What's the problem here?" I said.

"I didn't hit her," the driver said. His voice squeaked with fright. "I didn't. She came out of nowhere."

I glanced around. "Who?"

"She left. She wasn't hurt."

"So what's the problem?"

"I have this under control," the cop said. "Go away." He did not look friendly.

I was glad I had Deng at my back.

"He wants fifty pounds," the driver said. "Or he'll take my license."

"As the complainant has left the scene," I said, "this matter is over. You can be on your way. Give the man back his license."

The cop turned to me. He took a step forward. People began to edge away.

I held out my hand. "Ray Robertson."

He hesitated. I kept my hand extended. I looked into his face. I grinned like an idiot. At last, he took my hand in his. We shook, but I did not let go. I applied a bit of pressure. He was tall, but I was taller. And, I like to think, stronger willed. I pressed his hand and shuffled forward half a step. He stepped back. A couple more half steps and his butt was against the hood of the car. He tried to take his hand back, but I didn't release it.

"I hope we can resolve this," I said. "As friends. As fellow police officers. No harm done, eh?"

His eyes shifted. He saw the crowd of people watching us. Two guys having a friendly chat, getting on.

"We are finished," he said at last. "You may go."

I let go of his hand, but I didn't step away.

I waited.

He threw the license to the driver. "You go."

Then I stepped back. Everyone was smiling.

The driver leapt into his car. The engine turned. It stalled. He finally got it started and pulled into the stream of traffic. Dust and gravel sprayed behind it.

The cop gave me a big smile. He patted my shoulder. "Friends. Yes."

He sauntered away. The crowd dispersed and soon only Deng and I were standing on the side of the road.

"You take chances sometimes," Deng said. "It was only fifty pounds. Let their embassy pay."

My blood boiled.

"We don't ask for bribes. Not ever."
I began to give Deng a lecture on the value
of public trust in the police. Then I noticed
a twinkle in his eye. He knew. He just liked
to poke me now and again.

We went back to the truck.

Read to page 89

Page 75 due Thursday

CHAPTER ELEVEN

I don't want to give the impression that I'm a detective. I'm not. I'm just a uniformed officer. Back home, it was my job to keep the peace, hand out speeding tickets, break up Saturday night fights. When I got promoted to sergeant, I was put in charge of a platoon. I spent most of my time behind a desk, sending my officers onto the streets.

I'm not trained in questioning suspects or in spotting clues.

But here, in Juba, I was all I had to work with.

I decided to pay another call on the Blue Nile.

I told Deng I had a personal matter to attend to. He could pick me up for work later. He didn't ask what was up.

I waited until most of the dinner crowd would have left. Then I signed out a car and drove to the Blue Nile.

I didn't get very far. The guard at the gate recognized me. He dashed into his hut, probably to make a call.

The little waitress also recognized me. She'd served me Nile perch and told me the woman who owned a red glass earring was named Judy. Now she took one look at me and bolted for the back. But not before I saw her face. If she'd been a white woman, I'd have said the skin around her eye was black and blue. It was badly swollen.

I headed toward an empty table. The bar was busy. Four white women laughed too loudly, their voices harsh in the quiet night.

Most of the customers were men. A few couples perched on bar stools or sat close together at tables in dark corners. The couples were brown and white, white men with black women.

Nothing wrong with that. Nothing wrong with a lonely man wanting to meet a pretty woman either.

I was interested in what else might be for sale in the Blue Nile.

The manager came out before I got to a table. Two guards followed.

"Get out," he said. "You're banned."

"Hey." I lifted my hands in the air. "I'm just here to have a beer."

"I said you're banned. Now leave. Or I'll have you thrown out."

The guards took a step forward. All conversation around us died. The women stopped laughing. The people at the nearest table picked up their drinks and slipped away.

"Okay," I said. "I'll go someplace else."

"See that you do."

I turned and walked away. I could feel the guards' breath on the back of my neck all the way to my car.

CHAPTER TWELVE

When I got home from work the next morning, I was tired and grumpy.

Herding livestock isn't part of my job description. Shortly before sunrise, Deng and I had come across a frightened boy. He was running down a path in a shantytown on the city's outskirts. We stopped and Deng asked what was wrong. The boy explained that he'd lost the family's best goat. We drove slowly down the road, shining our flashlights into the bush. We didn't have to search long before we found it. The rope around the goat's neck had snagged on a thorny bush. It had spent its time productively. All the leaves and thorns within reach had been stripped off. We rescued the goat and returned it to the happy boy.

Heading back to the truck, I stepped in a hole. It wasn't a very big hole, but I didn't see it in the dark. I fell, my ankle twisting underneath me. Deng helped me to my feet, chuckling. It wasn't broken or sprained, but it was darn sore.

The sun was an orange glow in the eastern sky when Deng dropped me off at the UN compound. No one was around. I limped to my container, feeling very sorry for myself.

A length of measuring tape hung over my desk. I'd cut it off at thirty-one inches. Every morning for a month, I'd snipped off an inch. Eight inches were left. Eight mornings until Jenny and home.

I put my key in the lock and turned it. I pushed open the door and switched on the light. I'd untied the laces on my right boot to give the ankle some relief. Now I pulled both boots off. While I unfastened my belt, I limped across the room, heading for the small bathroom. I glanced toward my bed.

My heart just about stopped.

Eyes as white and frightened as a horse smelling fire stared back at me.

"What on earth?"

The face was small and round. Not from being well-fed but from baby fat. She was about twelve, maybe thirteen years old. Her hair was cut short. She wore dangling blue earrings. Her lips were painted bright red. Mascara had been thickly applied to her lashes. Her eyes blinked.

I crossed the room in two strides.

"Who the hell are you?" The duvet was pulled up to her chin. I grabbed the cover and yanked it down to her waist.

I leapt back.

She was naked. Nothing more than a bag of skin and bones. I could see her chest rising and falling. I could almost see her heart beating. Her breasts were no larger than peanuts.

"A present," she said. Her voice squeaked. Her smile was forced. "You like me?" Her accent was thick. The words spoken by rote. As if she didn't understand the meaning.

"Get up. Get up right now." My heart was beating almost as fast as hers. This was no present. Not a goodbye gift from my buddies. I looked around. Her clothes were draped over the desk chair. I scooped them up and threw them at her. "Get dressed."

Tears welled up in her dark eyes. "You don't like?" She tried to keep smiling. She pulled the duvet down, showing me a leg as thin as that of a stick insect. She cocked the leg. It wasn't seductive in the least.

"I most certainly don't like. Get up. Get dressed." I gestured to the clothes. "Now."

I turned and ran. I had the presence of mind to switch off the outdoor light as I fled.

I had no doubt someone was crouching in the bushes. With a camera. Ready to get a shot of the girl leaving my room. Hoping she'd be adjusting her clothes and I'd be half-dressed and grinning. I darted around the side of the container. I stopped to get some breath and to think. Not about who had done this. That could wait.

But about what I was going to do.

I could not be seen leaving my room with that poor frightened child. Camera or not, anyone could pass by at any moment.

Joyce lived two containers over. In off-hours she kept pretty much to herself. But she was friendly enough.

I pounded on Joyce's door.

"Keep your shirt on," she yelled.

The door opened. She peered out, blinking sleep out of her eyes. Her red hair stuck up in all directions. "Robertson. What's the matter?"

"I need your help. Now."

"I'm in bed. Can't it wait?"

"No."

She must have read something in my eyes. Pure panic, probably.

"Hold on." The door shut in my face.

It opened a minute later. She wore black track pants and was pulling a light jacket over her T-shirt.

"I got home a couple of minutes ago. I found something in my room," I said.

"What?"

"You'll see."

She stopped dead. "It's not a snake, is it? I can't stand snakes. You'll have to get someone else on this."

"Not a snake. No."

We went into my room. The girl was exactly where I'd left her. In my bed. Naked.

"Well, stone the crows," Joyce said in surprise. She turned to me. "You'd better not be having me on, mate."

"I swear. I walked through the door two minutes ago and found her. Right there. Like that."

"This isn't a joke," she said. "Someone's out to get you."

"I know."

She picked up the girl's shirt.

"Robertson, wait in the bathroom. You, time to get up."

I went into the bathroom. I heard Joyce ask the girl what her name was and where she lived. I couldn't hear the replies.

"You can come out now," Joyce called.

Dressed, the girl looked even younger. She wore a short skirt that jutted across bony hips. A low-cut, sparkly blouse revealed the top of barely-there breasts. Joyce held the girl's shoes in her hands. Gold sandals with thin straps and four-inch heels. I thought of my daughters. Dressing up as princesses for Halloween. Raiding their mother's closet to play dress-up.

This child was a travesty.

"We'll walk out together," Joyce said. "I'll hold the girl's arm, you come behind. Her name, by the way, is Olivia."

"And then what?"

"I'm taking her to an NGO that runs a shelter for war-orphan girls living on the streets. You're coming with us."

"You don't need me."

"I sure the hell do. Crikey, you think I don't know what some of your mates have to say about my supposed sexual orientation? I won't let them into my bed, so they figure I must be a lesbian."

I'd heard the talk. Figured it was none of my business.

"I've been married three times. I'm off men for the moment. Seemed like Africa would be a nice place to get away from my ex-husbands. I'm almost as vulnerable as you if I'm seen alone with this baby whore."

"Whore," Olivia said. "Yes."

"Let's go," Joyce said.

We snuck around the back rather than cross the compound in the open. Fortunately, it was still early. We didn't see anyone. The three of us marched into the motor pool. A driver was washing an SUV. Joyce told him she'd found the girl on the street outside. We were taking her to a shelter.

She pushed Olivia into the back of a Land Cruiser. Then she climbed in beside her.

I took the passenger seat. The driver said nothing.

As we drove through town we passed a primary school. Children were gathered in the dusty yard, kicking a soccer ball around. In Africa, any patch of ground and a group of kids means soccer. I've seen balls made out of plastic bags and string, bundles of cloth, even shredded car tires. The one these kids were playing with was white and black. A real ball. The children wore school uniforms.

Gray trousers and white shirts for the boys. Gray and black tunics over white shirts for the girls. The air might be full of red dust, but the uniforms were clean and well-kept. Parents who could afford school fees were determined to do the best for their kids.

The playing children burst into cheers. A boy ran across the yard, his arms in the air. His smile just about split his face.

I glanced in the back. Joyce was also looking out the window. She watched the laughing, playing children. She reached out and lightly stroked Olivia's hair.

Joyce took Olivia into the shelter for street children. I waited in the car.

Joyce soon came back. Alone.

We returned to the UN compound in silence. The schoolyard was empty. We could see rows of dark heads through the classroom windows.

"Thanks," I said as we walked to our containers.

"You've got an enemy, Ray. When men get to butting antlers, I stay out of the way. Your enemy used a little girl. I don't like that."

"It might turn out well for Olivia after all. She's better off in the home."

"For now. She'll be back on the streets soon enough. They can't keep them all, you know. There are too many girls without families. Too many blokes, white and black, ready to take advantage of that. And they wonder why I've gone off men."

She punched me in the arm. It hurt. I didn't want to look like a wimp by rubbing at it. "You're okay, Robertson. If this comes back to bite you, I'll back you up."

She crossed the thin weedy grass to her own container. Her steps strong and determined, her head straight. I was glad Joyce was in my corner.

I'd almost forgotten about my sore ankle. Now that the adrenaline was fading, the pain was returning. With it, a black rage.

Someone had tried to frame me. A couple of pictures sent to my bosses in Canada. Me leaving my room with an underage girl in the early hours. I could deny it until the cows came home. They might believe me. But the stench would linger for a very long time.

They didn't even need to send the pictures. Just knowing they were out there might be enough to have me minding my own business.

I ripped the sheets off my bed. I bundled them into the laundry basket. I remade the bed with clean ones.

CHAPTER THIRTEEN

Sleep didn't come. I lay awake wondering who had it in for me.

As a warning, it was a good one. No injuries, no violence. Just a message. Joyce had tried asking Olivia who'd brought her here. The girl didn't understand. Wouldn't have helped anyway. She wouldn't have been able to describe him with any accuracy. "They all," Joyce said, "look the same to these girls."

Since coming here, I hadn't made any enemies. Far as I knew. No one had ever tried a stunt like that on me or anyone else.

It had to have something to do with the events of the last two weeks.

Was someone trying to warn me off the investigation into the murder of the girls?

Why? It wasn't as if I was getting anywhere.

The people at the Blue Nile didn't like me much. Clearly, they'd rather I stopped poking around. That something funny was going on there wasn't in doubt. It might be nothing more than overcharging for drinks. It might be selling drugs on the side. It might just be that the manager was a weak guy who thought he was tough. They'd know where to find girls like Olivia.

Would they be able to get her into the compound? And into my room?

Possibly. With a few hefty, well-placed bribes.

Easier, though, if they had help from the inside.

It was no secret I was interested in the killings of the women. Everyone in the UN police and most of the South Sudanese knew. I'd been asking questions. Trying to open an investigation.

Was someone telling me to butt out?

I gave up trying to sleep. I had planned on making myself a special lunch that day. A big bowl of pasta. Might as well have it for a late breakfast.

I'd managed to score some butter at the store and arugula at the market. A woman who grew fresh herbs in her small patch of garden had given me a huge bunch. Fresh cream was unavailable. The milk would be out of a PVC pack. But you can't have everything.

I crossed the yard, dreaming of home-grown cherry tomatoes eaten warm from the sun. Nigel was heading toward me, dressed for work. He saw me, turned and walked away.

I called after him. He shouted over his shoulder, "I'm late, Robertson." He kept walking. I broke into a jog and soon caught up to him.

"What'd you do to your face?" I asked.

"Street brawl. You should see the other guy."

"You weren't working the last couple of days, were you?"

"I didn't say I was working. I said I was in a street brawl. Are all Canadians so bloody nosy?"

He stalked off. I let him go.

I'd seen enough.

Two long deep scratches ran down his right cheek. From the corner of his eye almost to his lip. Nasty. Half an inch over and he might have lost the eye. The injury wasn't fresh. Two days old, maybe.

Nigel was a hothead. It was entirely possible he'd been in a fight.

But he hadn't gotten those injuries in a punch-up. More like the result of a thin knife. Or a woman's long nails.

Nigel would know they didn't have the resources here to analyze blood for DNA.

But he would also know I'd try to secure the evidence anyway. As it was, I'd labeled the bag with the knife. I'd taken it into the police station and told them to keep it safe.

Tomorrow, my shifts switched to days. Nigel was working days also.

As I cooked lunch, I thought long and hard.

I scarcely tasted the pasta.

CHAPTER FOURTEEN

Nigel was a lot younger than me.

By the end of the fourth day, I was getting mighty tired. I worked with Deng during the day. I watched Nigel at night.

There isn't much of what we consider nightlife here. Police patrols come out around midnight. Roadblocks are set up. Cars are stopped by armed police for no reason at all. Most foreigners like to be home early.

Nigel was dating a British woman. He took her out to dinner one evening. I sat in the parking lot in my borrowed vehicle, watching the restaurant door. They went back to her place.

The other nights, he went out with male friends for dinner or a few beers. I showed the security guards my ID. I told them I was on a secret undercover mission. Whether they believed me or not, they let me wait in a dark corner of the parking lot. When Nigel left, I followed. He went straight back to the UN compound.

Sunday evening, the fourth night of my surveillance, Nigel went to a rugby game. Africa versus everyone else. He drank a lot of beer, chatted to women, didn't pay much attention to the game.

I lurked in the crowd. Feeling like a fool.

He never seemed to sense my presence. He didn't act like a man with anything to hide. There had been no further killings.

Everyone knew I was going back to Canada in a few days. Maybe he was waiting until I'd gone.

Or perhaps I *was* a fool, and Nigel had nothing to hide.

It was a slow, boring game. The score was tied. Only one player had been carried off the field on a stretcher. Nigel threw his beer bottle into a rubbish container. He slapped his buddies on the back and headed for the exit. I followed.

He hadn't driven himself. He'd been picked up. I wondered how he was planning to get home.

He exchanged greetings with the security guard at the entrance to the stadium. He crossed the parking lot, heading for the back where the lights were dim.

It was neatly done. If I hadn't been watching, I wouldn't have seen it.

A sharp jab to the driver's window. Probably with a rock he kept in his pocket.

Then the door was open and Nigel was inside. A quick duck under the dashboard and the engine started up. It was an older car. A battered Toyota Rav 4.

Nigel drove away.

I made it back to my own car in record time. I tore out of the parking lot after him. It was dark, not much traffic on the streets. I followed his rear lights at a distance.

He was driving fast, and I matched the pace. I bumped over rocks and into ruts. I careened around parked cars. Pop cans and water bottles crunched beneath my tires.

The car ahead turned onto a side road. I spun the wheel and followed. The road was unpaved, pitted with deep ruts alongside mounds of earth. Boda bodas swerved among the cars. I honked, telling them to stay out of my way. I kept my eyes fixed on the rear lights of the Rav 4. Easy to make out among the scooters and Land Cruisers.

This car needed new shocks. My back teeth rattled and I bounced up and down in the seat. It was like riding the moguls at Whistler.

Finally, the Rav 4 returned to a paved road.

Nigel stepped on the gas. I followed.

Then, out of nowhere, a pickup truck loaded with goats pulled out of a side street. I slammed on the brakes. I was driving too fast for road conditions. My car skidded, and I struggled to keep it under control. I jerked to a stop inches from the front of the truck. It had stopped square in the middle of the road. On either side, the ditch was deep. I'd never get around.

I rolled down my window. I shouted and waved my arms.

The truck driver waved back. Not in a friendly way.

The goats set up a chorus of *baah*.

The driver yelled insults that no doubt mentioned my parents. At last he shifted into gear and lumbered away.

I passed him, kicking up dust.

The Rav 4 had disappeared.

First I swore. Then I pulled out my phone. I called Deng.

"What's up?" he said. I heard a woman's low voice in the background.

"I've got him. Meet me at the Blue Nile. And make it fast." I snapped my phone shut and tore around the next corner. What Deng would make of that summons I didn't know. Would he come? If he was in bed with a woman?

I'd never been to Deng's house. I didn't know where he lived. I didn't know if he lived with anyone. I'd told him about my wife and daughters. I'd shown him pictures of them. He'd been polite and said they were beautiful.

We'd never sat down to have a meal together. We'd never socialized over a beer after work. He'd never been inside my container. He never so much as set foot out of the truck when he came to pick me up.

I knew almost nothing about him. But I trusted him. As a good man and as a good cop.

I couldn't search the entire city for Nigel. The Blue Nile was the only lead I had.

At least one of the dead women had worked there. They did not want me poking around. If the place had the reputation of hiring out its employees as prostitutes, Nigel would have no trouble getting a woman to leave with him.

But did it go further than that? Slip money to the owner. He wouldn't report that the woman never came back.

The country was in flux after twenty years of war. Refugees were returning.

Foreign workers poured across the borders in pursuit of jobs. Villagers came to the city in search of better lives. Many would soon turn around and go home. They had no ties here. No reason to tell anyone they were leaving.

If a prostitute didn't turn up at her regular spot again, no one would care.

Until one dumb Canadian cop started asking questions.

Traffic was less chaotic after dark than during the day. Most of the children and animals were off the streets. I shifted gears as I rounded a corner and sped up.

The parking lot of the Blue Nile was almost full. I drove slowly, trying to look as if I was searching for a spot.

Then I saw it. Parked close to the guard hut. A battered blue Toyota Rav 4.

I circled around and drove away. No point in trying to go in. If the guards were the same ones who'd thrown me out on my previous visits, they'd recognize me. I couldn't sit there watching Nigel's car either.

Chances were the guards were paid not to notice men leaving with women. They wouldn't want me interfering.

My phone rang.

Deng. "I'm almost there. Where are you?"

The restaurant was at the end of a long dirt road cut through the bush. A scattering of tukuls were shrouded in darkness. I pulled to the side of the road. A single headlight came my way. I flashed my lights.

Deng pulled up. He was on a boda boda.

I explained the situation. Nigel had stolen a car and he'd driven straight here. I was willing to bet good money that he was even now negotiating for a woman's favors.

I couldn't go into the restaurant. They'd throw me out in a heartbeat.

But Deng could.

Nigel knew Deng. But if Deng kept his head down and stuck to the shadows, Nigel wouldn't notice him.

Deng gave me one of his looks. Then he drove away in a spray of exhaust fumes and dust.

I turned the engine off. The thick hot air filled the car.

I listened to the night. Small yellow eyes glowed from the bush. Foliage rustled. Something screamed. The shriek was cut off in mid-note.

The occasional car went past, heading back to town. Laughter from the river. In one of the huts, a baby cried.

I waited a long time. Then I heard men shouting farewells and the roar of a motor-bike. Deng stopped beside me.

I smelled beer on his breath. Not much I could say about that. I had sent him undercover into a bar.

"He's there. Drinking with a woman. A South Sudanese woman. Young, pretty. Her smile is very false. You think this is it, Ray?"

"Yes, I do. I'm sure of it."

My gut churned. I was sure, all right.

"What do we do now?"

"That, my friend, is the sixty-four-thousand-dollar question."

"The what?"

"Never mind."

"This is the only road out," Deng said. "We wait. We follow."

"Suppose we lose them?"

"We know where he is going."

"Suppose, this once, he changes the routine?"

Deng shrugged. "You in the car. Me on the boda boda."

"I don't want to split up. He's going to be dangerous if cornered."

I thought for a long time. The bushes rustled. No matter what was out there, it was not the most dangerous animal in Africa.

"I won't use the woman as bait," I said at last. "Get in."

Deng pushed the bike off the road and into a clump of ragged bushes. It might be there when he got back. It might not.

I turned the vehicle around and headed to the Blue Nile.

I parked the car by the gate. Blocking the exit.

Deng and I climbed out. Lights were strong overhead. The guard swaggered over. "You are not allowed here. You must move your car."

"Tough," I replied. "This is police business."

He opened his mouth as if to argue. Deng growled. The guard changed his mind.

"We'll wait." I gestured to the guard hut. Just a shack to keep the rain off their heads.

"You'll wait with us." I didn't want him sneaking away to tell his boss. I could see only the one guard. The others must be patrolling the grounds. It was late. The car park was almost empty now.

The three of us went into the hut. There were two blue plastic chairs. I took one. I gestured to the guard to have a seat. Deng leaned on the wall by the door. He crossed his arms over his chest.

We didn't have long to wait.

A burst of female laugher had Deng and me glancing at each other. I got to my feet.

Nigel and a woman came down the path. Her secondhand dress was too tight for her lush figure. She tottered on her high heels. Nigel's hand gripped her arm. "Steady there, Ella," he said, and she giggled.

I held up my own hand. Telling the guard to shut up. Telling Deng to wait.

Wait and watch.

Nigel and the woman crossed the parking area. They reached the Rav 4. Ella staggered. Nigel opened the passenger door for her.

I signaled to Deng, and we stepped out of the hut.

"Nigel Farnsworth," Deng said. "I am arresting you for car theft."

"What the hell!" Nigel spun around. "Christ, not you again, Robertson. What, you're a vice cop now?"

"I was at the rugby game," I said. "I saw you hotwire this car. Of course, I immediately reported it to the police."

The woman's eyes blinked rapidly.

"Get lost," Deng said to her.

Ella didn't have to be told twice. She kicked off her shoes and darted into the bushes.

"You bastard," Nigel said. "You always have had it in for me. This car belongs to a friend of mine."

"We can sort it out at the station," I said.

People were gathering. The kitchen staff. Some of the waitresses. A few stragglers from the bar.

"This is an outrage," Nigel shouted. The restaurant manager broke through the circle of onlookers.

"What's the problem here?"

He looked at me. He looked at Deng. He reached into his pocket. "I'm sure we can find some way to settle this."

Deng growled.

Nigel moved. He didn't try to get away. No point in that. Nowhere to go except into the bush. He wouldn't last long there. He pulled a knife out of his belt. It was a good-sized camping knife. The blade, sharp and clean, flashed in the light. It came at me, slicing air, heading for my belly. Startled, I jumped back. I tripped on a rock. My sore ankle gave way. I went down. Guards, cooks, waitresses and drinkers scattered.

The restaurant manager squealed. My head hit the ground hard. My vision blurred. I shook my head to try to clear it.

Nigel bellowed and brought the knife down. A straight thrust. This time it was heading for my throat. Gravel cut into my hands as I scrambled backward.

Then the knife was rolling across the ground.

Deng's big hand was wrapped around Nigel's right wrist. With a sharp twist, the Englishman's arm was jerked up behind his back. He grunted in pain and dropped to his knees. He lifted his head. His eyes blazed at me. Spittle formed in the corners of his mouth. "Race traitor," he spat.

I felt hands on me, and one of the security guards lifted me to my feet. Now they were being helpful. The other guard bent to pick up the knife. I shouted at him to leave it where it was.

Once all danger had passed, the manager hurried over.

"What seems to be the problem, officer?" He rubbed his hands together. His smile was strained.

"Don't think I won't be back," I said. "I know what's been going on here. I know you're involved."

"You've completely misunderstood. I've never seen that man before." He shouted at the waitress who'd been beaten for talking to me. "He was with Ella. Find her. Make sure she's okay."

The waitress looked at me for a long time. She gave me a small nod. And then she slipped away.

"We'll be back," I said. "Regularly."

A clap of thunder sounded overhead. A drop of rain fell onto my hand.

Deng held Nigel on the ground. The Englishman's face was pressed into the dirt. "Get him up," I said. "And into the truck."

CHAPTER FIFTEEN

We took Nigel to the police station and charged him with car theft. He made phone calls to the head of the UN mission and the British embassy.

He didn't spend any time in jail.

Once the smirking Nigel had gone, I took Deng back to get his motorbike. We found it where he'd left it. He started up the engine and roared off into the night. Bolts of lightning lit up the dark sky, and the rain poured down.

I had not asked about the woman he'd been with when I phoned.

I'll never know if what I did that night was right.

Deng said nothing, but I knew I'd disappointed him.

He'd wanted to let Nigel drive the woman to the river. Wait until he was about to kill her. Then make the arrest. It wouldn't be so easy to get off a charge of attempted murder. With Nigel in jail, we could have started making the case for the other killings. Same place. Same MO. It should have been easy to prove, even in Juba.

I couldn't take that chance. If we'd lost him, Ella would have died.

I didn't see Nigel again. He was sent back to England right quick. A slap on the wrist for being so foolish as to be caught swiping a car.

His story was that he wanted to meet up with a woman and couldn't get a ride. So he stole a car. He would have returned it the next day. *No harm done, eh, mate?*

Nigel denied stealing Sven's Land Cruiser. I had no proof. It was never found. After using it, Nigel would have abandoned it on the backstreets and walked away. It would be in some remote town by now, being used as a taxi.

I searched Nigel's room. Unfortunately, he'd been allowed to pack one suitcase first.

I found a note among the remains of his things.

It didn't have my name on it. But I knew it was for me.

He'd drawn a smiley face in red ink.

A scrap of white ribbon lay beside it.

Serial killers don't spring up out of nowhere. There would have been incidents involving black women in Nigel's past. Unlikely, though, that they ended in murder. He took that big step knowing the risk of being caught was far less here.

A country without the resources to investigate human predators.

A country with only a few people to stand against the tide.

People like John Deng. Good people. People who needed help.

I'd done a lot of thinking while I waited outside the Blue Nile for Deng.

I thought about all that I miss here. My daughters. But they're adults and have lives of their own to live. Jenny, my wife, who I still love after all our years together. Lush green grass and towering old trees. Snow-topped mountains and clean air. Foggy mornings and soft rain. Flowers. How I miss flowers!

This was the heart of Africa. But so dry and dusty. Built up and polluted. There wasn't much color. A few foreign women planted pots of herbs and flowering shrubs. Some of the better restaurants stuck a couple of bougainvillea bushes outside. The flowers were soon covered in dust. The colors faded.

I missed working with men and women like me. With the same life experiences. Same dreams and disappointments.

Domestic disputes and runaway kids. Drunk drivers and car accidents. Bar brawls. Elderly people slipping on the ice.

Same stuff here. Except for slipping on the ice. But somehow, here, in this troubled land, I felt that I might be able to accomplish something. I wasn't just going through the motions anymore.

I sat down at my desk. I opened my email program.

I stared at the screen and thought for a long time.

I'd never told Nigel that I'd been to England a couple of years ago on anti-terrorist training. I'd met some officers from Scotland Yard. We'd spent a lot of time drinking in pubs and becoming friends. I'd kept in touch with a couple of them.

One was a woman who'd gone into Professional Standards.

Police investigating police.

I might just drop her a line.

But first I had a more important email to send. A much more difficult one.

I had to tell my wife I was going to put in for another year in South Sudan.

VICKI DELANY is one of Canada's most prolific and varied crime writers and is a national bestseller in the United States. She has written more than twenty-five books, and her work has been nominated for the Derringer, the Bony Blithe, the Ontario Library Association Golden Oak, and the Arthur Ellis Awards. Vicki's first book in the Rapid Reads series, *A Winter Kill*, features rookie constable Nicole Patterson. *White Sand Blues* and *Blue Water Hues* are the first two books in Vicki's latest series, featuring paramedic Ashley Grant. *Juba Good* is the first book in her Ray Robertson Mystery series. For more information, visit vickidelany.com.